PAULIE PASTRAMI ACHIEVES WORLD PEACE

by James Proimos

LITTLE, BROWN AND COMPANY
Books for Young Readers
New York   Boston

For Suzanne Collins, May We Never Drift Apart — J.P.

Little, Brown Books for Young Readers

Hachette Book Group
237 Park Avenue, New York, NY 10017
Visit our Web site at www.lb-kids.com

Little, Brown Books for Young Readers is a division of Hachette Book Group, Inc.
The Little, Brown name and logo are trademarks of Hachette Book Group, Inc.

First Edition: December 2009

Library of Congress Cataloging-in-Publication Data

Proimos, James.
    Paulie Pastrami achieves world peace / by James Proimos. —1st ed.
        p. cm.
    Summary: Seven-year-old Paulie, an ordinary boy, brings peace to his
home and school through small acts of kindness, but needs help to
achieve his goal of world peace.
    ISBN 978-0-316-03292-6
    [1. Conduct of life—Fiction. 2. Kindness—Fiction. 3. Peace—Fiction.]
I. Title.
    PZ7.P9432Pau 2009
    [E]-dc22
                                                2008043800

1010

10 9 8 7 6 5 4 3 2 1

Printed in China

The text is set in Cushing by Bitstream.
The display type is Gotham Condensed by Hoefler & Frere-Jones.

This is Paulie Pastrami.

He is eight years old now.

But he was only seven when

he achieved world peace.

Paulie Pastrami once ate an entire pizza in one sitting.

He beat a tiger in a race.

And he was even kissed by a girl.

BUT ACHIEVING
WORLD PEACE WAS
HIS GREATEST
ACCOMPLISHMENT
TO DATE.

How did he do it?

Paulie Pastrami was nothing special.

Certainly no more special than you are.

The kid had not yet mastered whistling.

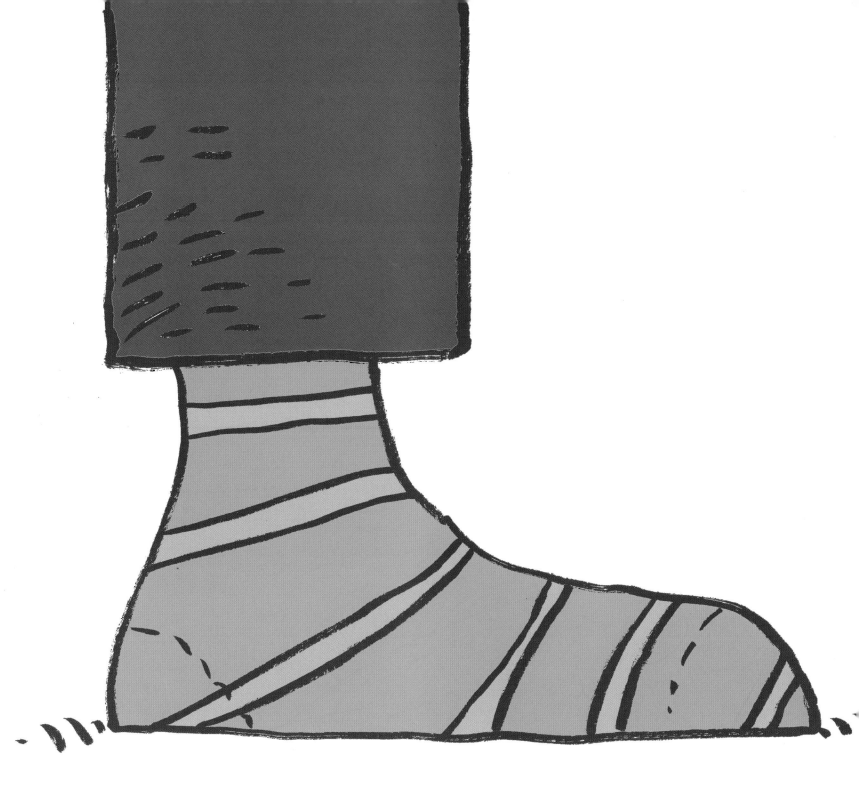

Often his socks did not match.

Paulie Pastrami was constantly picked last for street hockey.

HOW DID SUCH
A BOY ACHIEVE
WORLD PEACE?

Paulie Pastrami started by being kind
to small animals.

Then bigger animals.

And bigger.   And bigger still.

Next he tended to the earth.

Watering flowers . . .

Reading to trees . . .

And listening to the river

tell him stories of long ago.

Eventually, Paulie Pastrami turned his attention to mankind. He apologized to his little sister for something he did when he was five years old.

She was having none of it.

So he made her
the most fantastic
doll he could.

She immediately forgave him.

Next, Paulie Pastrami decided to take
his cause to the classroom.

He began to listen more . . .

Shared his lunch with Morris Klepnick when he forgot his . . .

And sang often.

Paulie Pastrami offered compassion to those in need.

He worked hard,

finished what he started,

laughed at himself,

and cried with others.

Paulie Pastrami learned

that a misunderstanding

could often be settled

with a **cupcake**.

Paulie Pastrami's actions had an impact on the entire classroom.

AHHHHHHH.

In fact, the whole school was at peace.

He was elected
class president,
class vice president,
hall monitor,
crossing guard,
birthday party coordinator,
and best person
on the planet.

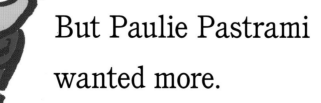

But Paulie Pastrami
wanted more.

He wanted WORLD peace.

Paulie Pastrami went to his parents.

"I MUST ACHIEVE
WORLD PEACE
BY TONIGHT,"
HE TOLD THEM.

"Hmmm," said his mother.

"Hmmm," said his father.

Then, his father said:

Off they went in their '68 VW Beetle.

First stop, Furniture World.

After that, it was on to Tire World.

Then, Sports World.

Next stop, Toy World.

Then, World of Magic.

Paulie Pastrami brought cupcakes
and peace to them all.

It wasn't until Paulie Pastrami handed
out cupcakes at Mattress World that he
realized how tired he was. So he and his
father called it a day.

When they got home, Paulie Pastrami's father made a big announcement.

WELL DONE.

Paulie Pastrami's mother applauded wildly.

That night, Paulie Pastrami's parents thanked the heavens that they were blessed with such an incredible boy.

And in his room, Paulie slept.

Peacefully.